Summer Color!

by Diana Murray

illustrated by Zoe Persico

L B

LITTLE, BROWN AND COMPANY
NEW YORK   BOSTON

The hot summer sun lights the sky like a torch
as folks fan themselves on the shady back porch.
The sparrows keep chirping a song, soft and mellow,
and sunflowers reach up with petals so Yellow.

Mama serves peaches and cold lemonade.
It's hard to stay cool, even here in the shade.
Daddy and Uncle bring chairs from the shed.
Our cousin shares ice pops, so swirly and red.

But far past our yard and the little stone well...

beyond the tall meadow where quiet deer dwell . . .

... and over the hill, where the willow trees sway,
the clouds in the sky turn a dark shade of gray.

The wind starts to stir. A few drops pitter-patter,
and critters that creep in the grass quickly scatter.
Rain batters down on the blustery scene,
as cardinals fly into treetops so green.

Splashing and splattering, streak after streak,
the rain soaks the earth and sweeps over the creek,
where frogs start to croak and the water snakes slink,
and wildflowers glisten with petals so pink.

It rains on the cliffs where the egrets take flight,
and down on the waterfall, misty and **white**.

It rains on the lake where the paddleboats rock,
and drenches the people who fish from the dock.

The picnickers pack up their salads and pie,
and run with their bright purple blankets held high.

It rains on the meadow where cozy mice hide . . .

... then *here*, in our yard ...
as we hurry inside!

Our soggy shoes squeak when we race through the door.
We crowd by the window and watch the rain pour.

It falls on the chairs and the swing set out back,
on the **brown** wooden fence

and the shed painted **black**.

A flash and a **CRASH** fill the thundery sky.
But we're snug in our soft orange towels—all dry.

The storm drifts away and reveals the bright sun.
We head to the yard for some more summer fun!

The rain left behind a refreshing, cool breeze, and silvery droplets that sparkle on trees,

and plenty of puddles for playing in, too—

and in each reflection . . .

...a clear sky of **blue**.

We skip and we jump, we twirl and we dash . . .
Our hot summer day . . .

...ends with a **SPLASH!**

For Danny and my sunshines,
Kate and Jane
—D. M.

To Lacey, you will always
be my ray of sunshine.
—Z. P.

The artwork for this book was designed using traditional-art-inspired digital brushes and media. The type is set in 17C Print and the display type is 17C Print. This book was edited by Allison Moore and designed by Jen Keenan with art direction from Saho Fujii. The production was supervised by Erika Schwartz, and the production editor was Annie McDonnell.